Benjamin Guilfoyle is a performance poet and primary school teacher based in Lancaster. He first began writing and preforming his own work in 2014 and since then things have gotten out of control.

His poetry has taken Benjamin all across the North of England where he has headlined poetry events and festivals.

'**Please insert disk 2**' is Benjamin's first poetry collection and is the follow up to his first publication, 'Level Up', which was released in 2015.

In 2019 Benjamin took his poetry on the road with 'The Wandering Poet Tour' where he performed 12 shows in 12 days in 12 different towns, walking all the way from Lancaster to Brighouse to raise money for the Lancaster Homeless Shelter and the Lancaster Children's Library.

Benjamin has also used his poetry to make the short film 'Pilate's' and a short, stop-motion animation, 'My Forest'.

Copyright © 2019 by Benjamin Guilfoyle

All rights reserved. No part of this book may be reproduced or used in any manner without written permission of the copyright owner except for the use of quotations in a book review.
For more information, address:
woollyhatpoems@gmail.com

The Right of Benjamin Guilfoyle to be identified as the author of this work in accordance with the Copyright, Designs and Patents Act 1988.

Cover image and all other illustrations in this book by Inés G. Labarta.
wonderlust.wordpress.com

IBSN: 978-1-78972-244-4
Independent Publishing Network

FIRST EDITION

www.facebook.com/woollyhatpoems

Please insert disk 2

by

Benjamin Guilfoyle

"Benjamin's poetry is often full of joy for geekery and niche pop culture, yet the poetry itself is far from niche. Accessible, warm, heartfelt and true, Benjamin only uses his love of video gaming and cult films as a vehicle for exploring universal aspects of life; loneliness, inequality, belonging, love, happiness and gratitude. It is a pleasure to immerse yourself in the world of words Benjamin creates, a not dissimilar experience to getting cheerfully lost with a movie or Playstation. A beautifully phrased and inspired collection."

Dominic Berry, No Tigers

"No matter what Benjamin chooses to write about, his poetry is always underscored by his infectious optimism and heart. Often inspired by his love for all things geek culture, his teaching and observations from his everyday life, Benjamin's work is unapologetically personal but never alienating. His words invite you into his world and you're more than happy to go along for the ride. 'Please insert disk 2' is often hilarious; often heart warming; and always brilliant."

Bróccán Tyzack-Carlin, Don't Bother

"A friendship bound by a collective love of hats, poetry, green tea and charitable stuff... Benjamin is a wonderfully unique, endearing, witty and inspirational 'Human Bean'. His 'words and rhymes' have a personal quality, full of warmth that reaches audiences of all ages. Every encounter is a life affirming, imaginative celebration of the universe. My only regret! I'm too old to squeak into, the early years class he teaches!!!"

Tony Gadd, Gong-Fu Poets

"Benjamin Guilfoyle's poetry packs a cosmic punch with a wide-eyed wallop. Subjects tackle the impotent rage inherent in a futile universe by dissecting society in microcosm, and celebrating with a fist punch, the micro victories that get us through the day. He's a joy to read and see."

Matt Panesh, The Monkey Poet

"Full of life, hope and individuality. Guilfoyle's poems depict the nuances in between the shuffle and the shout, and contain a grounded, endearing frankness common to the exciting new breed of northern poet. He also has the quality of being a poetic 'double threat'; brilliant live and brilliant to read. Please do both of the above, as quickly as you can, ta."

Geneviève L. Walsh, The Dance of a Thousand Losers

Contents

On your mark
On your mark
You
Library
Stargazer
f-o-n-i-x   f-ai-z   th-r-ee
Colin
Nick'd
Little Red

"Gordon's Alive!?"
Blessed be thy name
Precipice
My Forest
Songs of Sanctuary
Train Tourette's
Glass slides of a magic lantern
No change
Pilates

Just forget I was in Star Trek
I was touched by Patrick Stewart
Fresh
I choose you!
It makes no difference
Happy New Year
She

My suspension of disbelief
This is a cinema
12th century shower scene
Breaking up with George
A human is not an Etch A Sketch
The Batman
Mushroom revelations
Look stupid. Feel perfect.
Driftwood

Please insert disk 2
Please insert disk 2
The death and birth of John Connor
Level up
We are the people who sit at traffic lights
Horses in the wake
Farewell Honalee
Can you remember?

I will keep on dancing
Tea
Dear Tom Gorman
Evolve
I will keep on dancing
Beginning

'**Please insert disk 2**' is my first poetry collection.

42 poems.

Just as I was when I made my first poetry pamphlet '**Level Up**' in 2015 I am incredibly proud of this book and I have shocked myself by actually seeing it through to completion. There have been more than a few times where I have wanted to sack the whole thing off and play video games instead.

I'm not going to lie. I have worked really hard to make this book a reality. This book has sucked up an insane amount of hours from my life and for the most part it's been a fairly enjoyable experience.

This book wouldn't be a real thing without the help of **Inés G . Labarta** who has listened to my insane ramblings, taken my horrible, scribbly pictures and somehow turned them into the most magical illustrations. Thank you so much. This book wouldn't be a book without you.

Without **Diana Bebby** this book would be full of the most horrendous spelling mistakes and grammatical errors. Her proof reading skills are second to none. Thank you.

Thank you to **Dominic Berry** who has acted as an unofficial poetry mentor of sorts. He has guided and cheered me on through all of my poetic endeavours and I don't think I would be where I am today without him.

Finally, thank you to everyone who has seen me perform or read my poems over the past few years. My poetry would be nothing without you. You are all superstars!

"Mr Guilfoyle, the world is very big and we are very small, and even when we grow up we will still be very small and the world will still be very big. Even if we found a real life giant, even the giant would be very small, 'cos the world is just so big and around the world is space and in the space is rocks and stars and everything is just so big we just won't get time to see it all!"

- Louisa (6 years old)

For my niece,
Ivy Ruth.
The brightest of all the stars.

On your mark

Head up.
Eyes bright.
The road is long
and dark as night.

Find your own pace.
Keep a brave face.
Use what you learn
and you'll find your own way.

Grow up to be honest,
steadfast and true.
From here on out
it's all up to you.

But once you begin
your time won't slow.
Are you ready?

On your mark...

Get set..

Go.

You

The world is your stage
and everyone is waiting
for you to perform.

Don't be afraid.

Stand up tall.
Take a deep breath.
Then give this world hell!
Well..
at least
do your best.

Don't be put off
by the things that are ugly.
There are things that are mean
and there are things you can't
change.
Those things will upset you
and hurt you
and trip you
but
each time you fall
you will get up again.

Never forget
you are never alone.
You will figure out the rights
and the wrongs of this world.
You will carve your own path
and find your own feet
but you have to be strong
until you affirm for yourself
what is real

and when you find what is true
you won't need to believe
in pink or blue.
You will stand out
unique –
like everybody else.

You will believe in the things
that make you
you.

Library

She looks up.
Four floors.
She's never been in this library before
and it is big.

Really big.

Any other library is tiny
in comparison.
Intrepid and wide-eyed
she carries on
into the library. A paragon
of all she aims to stand upon.

Walking the corridors
of all four floors
completely in awe
she feels the bindings, smells the pages
and falls deeply in love

with each book. Portals to adventure
and enlightenment.
The library is a wonder of the world.
A true revelation.

She is deep inside a forest
constructed from knowledge.
Anything she could want to know at her fingertips.
All she has to do is forage.

For rich and magical are the trees
with spells printed on their leaves.
The shelves are sturdy; the books, evergreen.
She wants to get lost and never leave.

Stargazer

I climbed a tree.
I reached for a star.
My arms were too short.
The stars were too far.

Never discouraged and
full of hope
I borrowed my father's
telescope.

f-o-n-i-x f-ai-z th-r-ee

E-v-r-i m-or-n-i-ng a-f-t-er r-e-j-i-s-t-ur we d-oo
f-o-n-i-x a-n-d t-r-i-k-i w-er-d-z.

The s-ow-n-d-z we y-oo-z t-oo b-i-l-d w-er-d-z u-p
are c-or-l-d f-oa-n-ee-m-z.

We are d-oo-i-ng f-ai-z th-r-ee.

We are v-e-r-i g-u-d a-t b-i-l-d-i-ng
ow-er s-ow-n-d-z into w-er-d-z.

We are v-e-r-i g-u-d a-t b-i-l-d-i-ng
ow-er w-er-d-z into s-e-n-t-e-n-s-e-z.

D-oa-n-t f-or-g-e-t f-i-ng-er s-p-ai-s-z a-n-d f-oo-ll
s-t-o-p-z a-n-d c-a-p-i-t-ll l-e-t-er-z a-t the s-t-ar-t.

Ow-er t-ee-ch-er s-ai-z ow-er s-ow-n-d-z
are l-igh-ck l-e-g-oa p-ee-s-z a-n-d i-f we h-a-v
the r-igh-t s-ow-n-d-z we c-a-n b-i-l-d
e-n-ee-th-i-ng a-n-d s-ai e-n-ee-th-i-ng we w-o-n-t.

F-er-s-t we g-e-t a w-er-d
th-e-n we y-oo-z r-oa-b-o-t ar-m-z t-oo
ch-o-p u-p the w-er-d into s-ow-n-d-z a-n-d
th-e-n we s-ai the s-ow-n-d-z a-n-d
th-e-n we p-u-t the s-ow-n-d-z b-a-ck
t oo-g-e-th-er into w-er-d-z.

I-f y-oo f-igh-n-d a w-er-d th-a-t y-oo c-ar-n-t
ch-o-p up th-e-n th-a-t is a t-r-i-k-i w-er-d.

Ow-er t-ee-ch-er s-ai-z we j-u-s-t h-a-v to
l-ur-n th-e-m.

Oo i-z m-i-z-ch-ee-v-s b-ee-c-o-z i-t c-a-n b-ee an 'u' or an 'oo' s-ow-n-d.

I c-a-n h-ear the s-ow-n-d-s i-n my h-e-d a-n-d i-t h-e-l-p-s me to r-igh-t.

I l-igh-ck f-o-n-i-x a-n-d t-r-i-k-i w-er-d-z.

I a-m r-ee-l-i g-oo-d a-t r-igh-t-i-ng.

Colin

"Sir! It's Colin.
He fell an' scraped 'is knee.
Now he won't stop sobbin so
we came t'you t'see
if you could help t'stop the bleedin'.
Blood's pourin' down 'is leg.
Y'can almost see the bone, Sir!
It's a nasty, bloody mess.
Y'can see the trail he's left.
Like breadcrumbs - but it's not.
It's blood.
It's in't carpet, Sir!
I just don't know what t'do t'help.
Right, I just saw 'im.
He wer' chargin' straight at me.
An' I wer' playin' king's guard
an' the king's guard guards the keep.
An' Colin wer' a bad guy on a mission
while 'is team tried drawin' mi attention
so I wun't see Colin creep
toward the castle keep.
The sneaky little creep!
He tried t'steal the treasure, Sir,
the dirty little thief!
But, Sir, it wan't my fault,
it wer' Jacob from class three.
He told me t'do it, Sir,
an' I follow orders, me,

see, y'don't say no t'Jacob
wen Jacob's playin' king and,
Sir! I'm only in year two
an' Jacob's really big.
But he saw Colin comin'
an' he said that it'd be funny
if Colin 'took a trip' so that he wun't steal our money
and, Sir, I didn't mean it, Sir!
I know I've bin' a twit.
But, Sir, I stuck mi leg out
an' I watched as Colin hit
the tarmac on t'playground floor,
I saw
'is body slid.
It wer' like it wer' in slow motion, Sir,
and he bit 'is lip!

Please, Sir, don't be angry,
can't you see I didn't mean
for Colin's blood t'form a trail right back t'scene?
From the staffroom t'playground
t'unforgivin' stained ground
where Colin's blood an' 'arf 'is knee
as found him playground fame! Now, Sir!
That's t'whole story
an' I'm really, really sorry.
What can you do about Colin's knee?
It's lookin' kinda' gory
an' for all 'is playground glory
Colin's lookin' kinda pale.
Should he really be stood up, Sir?
Shall I sit 'im at that table?

Come on, Sir! Say sommat!
Just tell me what t'do.
Is Colin gonna die, Sir?
D'ya think that he'll pull through?
D'ya think he'll be
an amputee
with a massive piece o'dowel
stickin' out from where 'is leg once was?
Like a pirate with a scowl?
A hook hand an' a hobble?
I can picture it right now, he'll
look like a cross breed of James Hook,
Black Beard and Captain Sparrow!
Long John Silver too, wi' wooden leg.
I'm just sick of 'earin' 'im howl.

Shall we just do what we always do
and get a wet paper towel?"

Nick'd

I watched
as you placed the blade to your neck
and with a surgeon's precision
you began to cut.

I dare not breathe.
You teetered on the edge of life and death
so cool and calm
with a concentration for the ages.

The unthinkable happens.

A sharp intake of breath.
A spattering of red.
A blade dropped.
A hand to your neck.

The crimson water filtered through your fingers

and you were not scared.
You were brave.
I'll be brave too
when I learn to shave.

Little Red

Little Red
saw the bed.
The bed was red.
Granny was dead.
What was left?
Just a head.
The wolf was fed.
Red was next.

— "GORDON'S ALIVE!?" —

I was front row. Centre seat.

Brian Blessed took to the stage. Larger than life.
The living mountain.

He studied the audience and took a deep breath.

"GORDON'S ALIVE!?"

We whooped, we cheered, we clapped, we whooped some more.
Flash Gordon. 1980. Classic.

Brian scaled the face of Everest! Brian was in Star Wars! Brian survived a plane crash **and then** led an expedition into the unexplored jungles of Venezuela! Brian saved an endangered species! Brian became an astronaut!

"..we are all but children of stardust.." he said. "Take pleasure in the smallest things, because the very fact that we even exist is the most beautiful of coincidences."

Blessed be thy name

Child of stardust
roar large and roar loud.
Let the whole universe hear your voice
raw with power
from the very depths of your soul.
Dig in deep.
Be immoveable. Root your feet
and be a mountain.
Scrape the edge of space.
Dance with the stars and blaze
a trail of kindness
into tomorrow's uncertainty.

Be an unstoppable force.
Gain momentum with every step
and with every breath
breathe deep
until those lungs are fit to burst.
Climb for your dreams and believe
that there is nothing you can't attain.

Don't let the bastards grind you down!

Be a gentle thunder.
As mighty as Zeus
with compassion beyond measure.
And when you sit on top of your Everest
and weep at the beauty of the cosmos
it is not because
you are tiny
but because you are a giant
and you have so much left to explore.

And when Death comes
you will stare it down and say
"No!
Not today!"

Because you will have made yourself an immortal
and Blessed be thy name.

Precipice

The precipice is
the edge of all things.

That's where she sits
with her arms round her shins.

She loves it where
she can breathe in
the freshest of air
as she bathes in the wind
and it blows through her hair.

Grass between toes
because she prefers
to have her feet bare.

No one else knows
that this place exists.

Her place to escape.
Her own precipice.

My forest

This is my forest.
I've known it all my life.
I know all its nooks and secrets
look!
I'll show you -
if you'd like?

Take my hand. I'll take the lead.
I'll show you things you cannot see
with city eyes –
so follow me.

Ancient trees and mossy rocks
I'll show you how to climb and cross.
The fallen trees we'll stoop beneath.
We'll smell the freshly rained-on leaves.
We'll pick up sticks and make believe -
like fresh green tea!

Don't you find it refreshing?
Cleansing? Soothing?
Take a deep breath in!
Hold up those nostrils.
Savour the scent!
Potent. Ancient. Peaceful
and yet
it's busy. Bursting and bustling with life
and if you look hard enough
with the right sort of eyes
you'll see more than just trees.
You'll see Gaia. Divine.

Because this is her forest.
It's not really mine.

Songs of Sanctuary

I hear the distant drumming;
that beat. It's infectious.
Vibrating through every joint
with warmth. A connection.
A searing heat.
A burning heart extends
through tribal hands that reach.

Colours twist and burn in the fire.
Naked feet beat hardened peat
encompassing the pyre.
Flames lick higher
and dance around the incandescence.
They chant aloud in evanescent tongues.
No human ear can understand these songs.

Throngs of bodies contort.
Adoring arms are thrown to the sky
while songs take place of a sacrifice
and whatever gods remain
are appeased.
They dance through the night
under ancient trees.

Sunrise pierces dense vegetation.
Morning breathes life into the ancient forest
now heavy with the burden of time.
A once-grand civilisation now desolate.
Ruined.
Enveloped in vines. The Earth's fingers
intertwined and curled
bringing order to the shadows of a forgotten world.

I have listened to Songs of Sanctuary.
I have closed my eyes and been given life anew
in a world where peace is eternal
and nature presides.

Train Tourette's

Any time we were out anywhere
or we were going somewhere in the car
or there was one on the TV
or we could hear one in the distance behind the trees
or in the background of an illustration of a book
we'd be sharing with me on your knee
you would always say:

"Ben! Train!"

and you still do it to this very day
and I'm thirty-two now.
If you see one and you think I've not
you'll say it:

"Ben! Train!"

My head will turn
and I'll stop and watch until the last wagon has gone.
I'll crane my neck
to get a glimpse from the car window.

It's like a magic spell

and I do it now when I'm at work with the kids.
"Children! Quick! Look! Train!"
"I wonder where it's going?"
"Look at all those wagons. Let's count how many there are!"
"Ooh, it's pulling carriages today.
That'll be a passenger train, that one."
And I'm sure they're sick of it but I can't help it.

Train Tourette's.

But it didn't stop at the trains.
Through Thunderbirds, Ninja Turtles,
Power Rangers and Star Wars
you would point it all out.

Books, posters, TV spots
and collect the token special offers
on the Weetabix box.
You knew what I loved, what made me tick,
and you didn't think twice
from day one through my entire life –

and you didn't have to.
But you did
and I appreciate it.

So thank you.

Glass slides of a magic lantern

When all is darkness
with fire we shine.
Like pinholes in the curtain of night
we illuminate
dead eyes.

We are adventure,
fairy tales,
mystery.
We are magic,
we are glass,
we are history.
Consistently splendid.
Our colour forever suspended
animation.
Liberation for the friendless.
We are timeless.
Endless.

Unless,
of course,
we are dropped.

No change

He feels like he could take on the world.
The guy behind the counter knows it.

Look at his face.
He is smug.
Head held high as he starts
to strut across the forecourt.

Give it up for this guy!

He needs banners, balloons,
streamers! STAT!
A party in the street
and a big party hat.

He has done the impossible!
Pulled off a feat that was never thought possible!

He has single-handedly stopped
the petrol counter thingy.
Quite precisely!
Bang on the dot!
Twenty pounds exactly!
Today he is winning!

And now he can pay
with a fresh note.

Boom.

No change.

Pilates

There are fifteen of us.
Real men. Paragons of humankind.
Proper hard core.
Each week we meet in the village hall
with a mat, a cushion,
a ball
and a will of steel.

We tuck in our tummies.
Work from our bottoms
and feel
muscles
we've never felt before.

Working towards a hard core.
We are an army division. The hard corps.
We grunt and let the sweat pour.
We glisten.
Phwoar!

We quickly realise we are not as hard as we once thought
as we fail
rather spectacularly
to get our legs into the double table top position
while keeping our centres stable, strong
with buttocks firm on the floor.
Ribs down and shoulders dropped.
Are we soldiers? Um...
I think not.

We tell ourselves it won't be long.
We suck it up,
we don't give up.
All of us. Every one.

We soldier on
because

resistance
is
futile.

Pilates
is
brutal

but we endure the agony.
The torment.
We become friends with the burn
and learn
that the more we keep our ass cheeks firm
the more the brutal
becomes
fruitful.
It's really
rather
beautiful.

Fifteen out of shape men,
contorting into some strange,
pulsating, sweaty mass,
writhing in pain
on the village hall floor.

Pilates will
kick
your
ass

and I couldn't recommend it enough.

— JUST FORGET I WAS IN STAR TREK —

Yeah?

Well, do you know what, Patrick? That's a pretty difficult thing to do. I used to run home from school to watch you on TV commanding the USS Enterprise. Boldly going where no man had gone before and now you're standing in front of me telling me to *just forget it*? I'm trying to remember this bloody Shakespeare monologue for you and I'm not a great fan of Shakespeare and my heart is pounding and I'm possibly having a heart attack and people are watching us.

I can't *just forget it*, Patrick!

I'm a good performer, I am, but you're standing there like an English oak and it's the most surreal thing that's ever happened to me.

I'm bricking it, Patrick.

Good God, man.

I was touched by Patrick Stewart

You heard.
Patrick Stewart touched me.
THE Patrick Stewart.
Patrick 'I was in Star Trek and X-Men' Stewart
touched me.
With both of his hands.
In front of an audience.

My god. It was amazing.

Oh no! Not like that!
Gosh no!
Not in some sort of grubby dirty pervy voyeur sort of way.
No! He was a gentleman.
Good as gold, he was.
Really super. Really lovely
and he walked up to me
- honest, he did -
and I was dead nervous, I was,
and he walked up to me
and he put his hands on my shoulders
and he looked deep into my eyes
and he spoke to me in that rich mahogany voice of his
and said:

"Just forget I was in Star Trek.
Pretend I wasn't in X-Men
and just see me,
for the next five minutes,
as your teacher."

And I did.

And he was.

And instantly all was right with the world.
There was this perfect calm like I'd overdosed on camomile
and for those five minutes my life was complete.
My acting technique was the worst it's ever been
and to this day I have no idea how I was able to talk myself into
an acting masterclass with Patrick Stewart
but I did

and I can't prove it.

We weren't allowed to take photographs
but it really did happen.
One of the best days of my life it was.
I met my childhood hero.
The man I used to run home from school to watch
command the USS Enterprise.
Patrick Stewart.

He touched me.

And it was wonderful.

Fresh

I can't express the joy I feel
as teeth rip into your skin.

Your outer shell
is breached
and your dry flakes fall.
Ah!
That fresh scent fills my nostrils.
I love how your innards are still warm.

Lifeless
you flop.
Thinner.
A sliver.
Your purpose in life
was to be my dinner
and I am the hand that guides.

You have fulfilled your destiny.
In the end
you were more than just bread to me.

You were a loaf.
You were fresh from the oven.

I choose you!

To me
you are
the very best.

Possibly the best there ever was.

Out of sheer respect
I choose you.
Let's become one.
Let's connect.
Let's be stronger than infrared.
For you I'm prepped to take that step
and together...
YES!
We can get
to the next level.

Isn't that where you want to be?
Wouldn't you want to go there with me?

If that's too much
just say no.
I'll pack up my stuff and you can go

blasting off again
like every other playtime.

But if that's not the case
and I've got it wrong...
insert the link cable,
turn the Gameboy on
and we will sit down as trainers
and trade Pokémon.

It makes no difference

It makes no difference
what you have emblazoned across your chest.
I don't care which shoes go best
or whether or not they're the right shade of red to match
the bag in your hand and the scarf round your neck.

It makes no difference. You don't have to try.
I'm constantly impressed
just by the fact you're still here.
That somehow in this crazy old mixed-up universe of ours
you and I ooze the same brand of grade A insane.
It's mental.
By design or cosmically coincidental?

It makes no difference.
Just think of the potential.
What was once acapella is now instrumental
with bonus tracks
and a poster and a badge
and front row seats and a backstage pass.

It makes no difference
and I have no clue
as to why you stick around
and put up with me in the way that you do
but I'm glad you do.
'Cos me and you just about manage

to make a chilli con carne
that's 50% magic
and 50% carnage
and at times it feels like we're chasing a rabbit.
'Cos at times it feels like unsolicited madness

but it makes no difference.

And we are very different
but we're on a journey to find the brightest star.
It's all pretty stellar.
We will sit on a meteor hand in hand.
Sipping gin.
With our feet up watching Stranger Things
knowing full well this is one of the stranger things
to ever happen.

But it makes no difference

because you are Earl Grey tea to Jean Luc Picard.
You are the piano in Ben Folds Five.
You are the Death Star plans to the Rebel Alliance
and the weird thing is that you don't even try.
It just kinda works and that's kinda nice.

So it makes no difference
what's emblazoned across your chest.
'Cos I'm speaking from the heart.
and I think you're the best.

Happy New Year

Contrary to Girl's intoxicated belief,
Boy on the floor is awake.
Boy is in love with her.

Boy hears everything
as she asks if **he** would like to sit on her bed.

Bed sheets drunkenly fumbled.
The sound of lips touching.

Boy feels an unbridled pain as
his heart shatters
like a football shatters glass.

Boy wants to stand up
but
he lies there listening,
breathing,
seething,
angrier than he's ever been
and his only vent
is a fist; clenched
as he lies
face down
on frozen remains
of a foolish endeavour.

It would be easy
to dispel the rage
but Boy isn't like that.
She knows it.

Eternity passes. She and he sleep.

Boy stands
and steps over the sea of the passed out.
He leaves the party.
New Year's morning hits like a fresh brick
to the face.

It
is
magic.

Anger transforms into
the strangest sense
of clarity.

She

She is the sunshine.

Of course, like everyone else,
She has her moments of rain.

She is the walk in the woods meant only for princesses
and every step She takes sees flowers bloom in her wake.

She is the path that forks in uncountable directions
and you know
without any shred of doubt
that every path leads to adventure.

She **IS** the adventure.
She is the very essence of excitement
and She will find discovery in everything
and She wants nothing more
than to share it
with
you.

She is a gentle giant.
She is everything you forgot how to be.
All the chances you didn't have the courage to take.

She is a fresh batch of hope
and a new head of dreams.

Now,
there are those days when the weather man
gets it disastrously wrong
and you don't take a coat
and get caught in the downpour
and your umbrella breaks more
cos it was already broke
and gets blown inside out
upside down
the wrong way round
and you realise that your life is a joke
but She...

She is the light that breaks through.

She is that extra log on the fire.
A hot cup of cocoa
a blanket and a cuddle.

She is your family.
She is alive
and She is just the best little person.

She is She.
She just
simply
is.

And you have said **no** to her.

It seems to me that there was a time where
if 40,000 leagues of sea
were to come between you and she
then no one else but you would be
the one to swim across

but now
you see

your keys are forever lost.
You are forever locked out in the rain.
Now every traffic light is against you

and I am the least religious person
but I hope and I pray
that whatever it is that you have found
that has made you turn away
is worth it.

— MY SUSPENSION OF DISBELIEF —

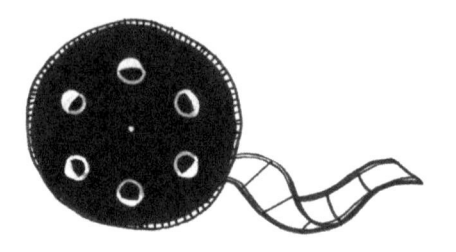

Yes.

This is most certainly a First World problem.

No.

I do not care if I cause you great embarrassment.

If you are:

- talking **or** whispering
- eating **or** rustling
- playing on your smart phone

at any point during the feature presentation

(that's any time after the trailers)

I will turn around and tell you,

politely,

- to shut your mouth
- choke on your snacks
- put your bloody phone away

How **dare** you ruin **my** cinema-going experience?

This is a cinema

Muscles tighten and shake.
The ripple of anger
pulsates and grows
through my entire body.
The toes curl.
The teeth grind.
The face contorts
and fury rises.

I
am
going
blind
with the purest
red
rage.

I fixate
on the incessant,
relentless
rustling,
crunching,
while developing Spiderman-esque abilities.
Heightened senses
pinpoint
the origin of the munching.

This is a cinema,
not a Greggs.
Do not bring your lunch in.

I paid to watch a movie,
not to hear you munch your luncheon.

I could leap from my seat and start blindly
punching
but my fingers curl. Nails dig deep
into the upholstery
to stop me from erupting,
exploding and confronting
whoever it is
two rows back and
three seats left
who thought it would be a grand idea to
bring the world's biggest bag of Doritos
into the film.

Don't misunderstand,
I realise that the cinema is a public place
but my suspension of disbelief
has now unequivocally
buggered off.
It's a disgrace.
The movie is as good as ruined.

I am not a rich man.
I will not get that back.
The £7.99
I paid for my ticket!

It's every single time.

I'm sick of it.

12th century shower scene

Well..
You wouldn't really call it a 'shower scene'.
It's only 39 seconds long
and it's not obscene
but
in Robin Hood: Prince of Thieves
there is a scene
where Robin,
played by Hollywood superstar Kevin Costner,
is totally starkers.
Chest and back and bum and balls
getting scrubbed beneath a waterfall
and if you squint
you can see it all..

Probably..

And it's good. A good scene. People need to wash.
You don't often see that in movies.
It's fine.
It's hygienic.

It's 1180AD-ish
and Marian (Maid) and her aide
decide to pay
Robin a rather impetuous visit
while he's enjoying a skinny dip / shower.
Which is fine.

It's superb.
No problems so far.

Marian turns. She has a look.
She sees his bum. A cheeky blush.

Refuses to look away of course
and that is fine. The girl's in love
and I bet that given half a chance
she would stand and stare
until the end of time
or at least until she got bored.
Whichever came first.

No such luck as a
gung-ho merry man calls out to Robin:
"ROBIN! YOU'VE GOT VISITORS!"

This is where the problem begins.
This is the shot that makes me cringe
harder than anything
and *I think*
this movie
is almost perfect.

Robin is wet.
Dripping. Sodden.
It's not a sunny day so I'm assuming he's cold
and he just
pops his pants back on.

His 12th century,
grubby,
rough,
tight-fitting
leather pants
back on without drying off.

I grimace.
He doesn't wear underwear. He is full commando
and that,
my friends,
is going to chafe.

It is nails on a chalkboard and
it pains me to the core.
You know when you get your fingernail caught
and it bends back?
That is what this scene does to me.
I want to throw a towel through the screen
Like that movie 'The Ring' but in reverse.
Dry yourself off, you poncey berk.

Other than that it's a top film.
Starring Morgan Freeman, Alan Rickman and
a cheeky appearance from Brian Blessed.
Chafing aside it's a 10/10.
Would definitely recommend.

Breaking up with George

Look, right,
I'm not having a pop.
I'm not that sort of person
and anyway
I don't think I've got the right words
to get my point across.

But

after all these years
I am still hurt.
Whatever it was that you tried to do
didn't work.

I am tired. Numb. Bitter.
Lost. I am
past being cross.
I'm just disappointed.

You held perfection in your hands
and you threw it away
like it was nothing.

It was the mystery that I liked.
It sparked my imagination.
We went on adventures without limitation!

We were liberated!
We were a perfect cadence
that once was tasted
left us wanting more.
Like heroin...
...or Pringles.

Now it's not hatred.
It's something pure.
There is a darkness inside
and you opened the door.

You were the petrichor.
You were fresh air
with a heart and
because you cared we cared too.
So thank you. I guess.
Because of you
we were empowered.
You took uncountable
hours from our childhoods
and that has not been time wasted.
We are glad that we did.

But Mr Lucas. George.
'Star Wars Episode Two:
Attack of the Clones'
was an atrocity
you didn't have to commit.

A human is not an etch-a-sketch

Grandad just didn't understand.
He was from a different time.

A boy loving a boy or a girl loving a girl
didn't work for him
and to a point, that was fine.

"Grandad!
They are not yours!
My feelings are mine!"

In the old man's mind
experimentation should be confined
to the lab.
A weird science.
Behind locked doors.
Out of sight... Out of mind...

In his head
two boys kissing
was, like, Nazi-level bad.
Against the natural order of things.
A mental disorder. Discordance of genes
that creates the flamboyant performance of queens.

Now Grandad was dead.
Not one tear did he squeeze from his head,
for a human is not an Etch A Sketch.
He couldn't shake away the memories
like you'd wipe a cassette
and as the man looked back over tattered shreds
of memories etched
in the walls of his heart
there were just some things that he couldn't forget.

Like Grandad playing the judge.
With all of his prejudice
neatly gathered in a fist
pent up
poised to punch the boy in the face.

The Batman

Batman.

He wants to be Batman.

The Batman.

On an autumn night
when leaves cover the road
he begins to hum that classic soundtrack.

<begin to hum Batman 1989 opening theme here>
dooo do do doo doooo
Dooo do do doo do doooo
Dumm! Ptum! Ptum! Ptum! Ptum! Ptum! Ptum!
bad-a-ba baaaa
Dumm! Ptum! Ptum! Ptum! Ptum! Ptum! Ptum!

He puts his foot down.

The clapped out Citroën transforms
into the Batmobile!
Armour plates, grappling hooks,
the fiery exhaust by the rear wheels.
It's Batman turning the steering wheel!
In his mind it's that real.
This is a man who needs to feel
alive.

So he lives another life.
Locked behind invisible walls.
Safe encased inside his mind.
An imagination running wild
at crazy speeds
so he speeds..

Not too fast.

But fast enough for the thrill
and for a second
he believes.

The Citroën mounts and stalls on the pavement.
Black smoke splutters from the burnt-out exhaust.
He wonders where the day went.
Eyeing the four pound wine in the plastic carafe
on the passenger seat. A pathetic investment.
Just crack the top and neck it.

He knows he is not Bruce Wayne.
The truth says: sad case.
His home is not a Batcave
and a far throw from Wayne Manor.

No millionaire's riches
No parties. No swagger.
Just eternal fatigue.
Just what the hell happened?
He didn't even know anyone called Alfred.

It was a lie. All of it,
because The Batman is the one who hid
his real face behind a mask.
Eyes wide the man cries
into cheap wine.
Took this long to realise.
He didn't need to fantasise.

He already is The Batman.

Mushroom revelations

3.15 am.
Back in the land of the living.
He wakes up as if for the very first time.
The filthy Birmingham air never tasted so
clean.
Was it something to do with the things that he'd seen?
Maybe to do
with the five dried grams
of mushrooms he'd eaten?

Whatever.

His pride had taken a serious wound.
Slightly shabby. Slightly bruised
yet somehow undefeated.
Stripped of all his street cred.
He didn't feel victorious.
How could it be glorious
when freezing on the street
with a fading euphoria and tingling teeth
and blood on his sweater
that dripped
from where he'd been biting his cheek?

Anything but glorious.

But that's just how this story is.
Those mushrooms caused an epiphany
and kick-started metamorphosis
so he could choose a new path
like Neo did with Morpheus.

He was not 'The One'.

But he had ridden a wave on the edge of time.
Been chewed up, spat out
and come around shaken but more or less fine.
He had seen the infinite
and seen how beautifully insignificant
everybody really was.

Clenching his fist he dried his eyes
on the cuff of the jumper twice his size

as the sunrise scorched. Shrivelled starving
pupils squinted and burned in the new day.

Pretending his face was made of clay
he sculpted up his bravest face
and made his way
home. A complete
and utter
wreck
but with
a mind
that was
his own.

Look stupid. Feel perfect.

Please, gentlemen, please.
Calm down.
Don't panic.
Everything is going to be fine.
There is no need to feel embarrassed.
It's the 21st century and you deserve to feel empowered,
enhanced and ever so fabulous.
Why should you miss out on all the fun?
You think it's just for the ladies
and those with an effeminate persuasion?
Absolutely not.
You couldn't be more wrong.
You could look as gallant as Lancelot
with your skin as smooth as a natural yoghurt.
As soft and solemn as fallen blossom
with light and freshness radiating from every pore.
Take a good look at yourself! Are you not a man?
You could be so much more than a stereotype!
You don't have to be macho.
It's not worth the hype.
It's a load of old rubbish.
I wouldn't try to push this if I didn't believe it
but this is something I believe in.
Do yourself a favour.
Do a facemask. Start gleaming
because you should be beaming like a goddamn lighthouse.

You could be feeling like a god. Most highbrow
because you are not worthless.
You are worth it.
You are not just 'Mr DIY',
you are golden, friend.
You've earned it.
You are beautiful.
Take some downtime.
Put your feet up, you deserve it
and for 15 minutes a facemask
will make you look stupid
but feel perfect.

Driftwood

Battered, beaten and spat out
by the very storm that you created.
That you ran into.
Never thinking of the consequences.

Your splintered edges were
fit to rip
skin to strips.
Now your teeth that bit
and your voice that tore
is raw no more.

But

like the storm, you calmed.
You forgot how to roar.

We all watched as you
washed up on the shore.
Washed up. But sure.

You were alone. You were free.
You were simple and clean.
You were nothing more than driftwood
that finally drifted home.

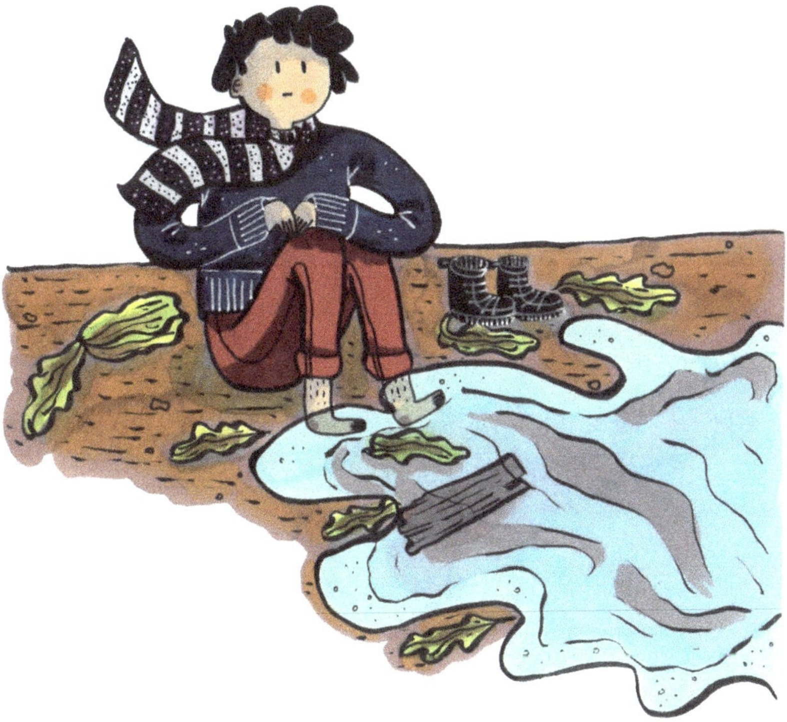

— PLEASE INSERT DISK 2 —

Some stories take a while to finish.

You remember playing those 70+ hour role-playing games on the Sony PlayStation and SEGA Dreamcast? Those ones with the epic stories that would span across two, three or even four disks?

They were great weren't they?

So many hours. So many memories.

My point is this. These games were long **but** if you persevered you would reach the "Please insert disk #" screen.

It meant that you had levelled up and built your character into a survivor.

The continuation of your story, the next stages and the unknown were only a disk swap away. It was always exciting...

but...

Disk two was new challenges. Disk two was always brutal.

<u>Please insert disk two</u>

Would you like to save?

This is the end of disk one.

Please insert disk two.

The death and birth of John Connor
(a poem that probably works better if you've seen the movie..)

If you've seen the movie
then you'll know what I'm talking about.
In the 1991 James Cameron movie 'Terminator 2: Judgement Day'
there is a scene early on where
the protagonist, John Connor,
dies a brutal and unforgiving death
as he is mercilessly crushed under the front wheels of a menacing
1987 Freightliner tow truck.

However,
if you have seen the movie
you will also remember that John Connor doesn't actually
get crushed to death by a tow truck.
John actually survives the whole movie,
the savage onslaught of the tow truck *and*
its driver, the relentless, time-traveling
assassin, the 'T-1000'
prototype model Terminator.

Allow me to explain.

Unbeknownst to John is that one day he will be a great hero.
The leader of the resistance against the machines.
Also unbeknownst to John is that right now
he is a motorbike.
His motorbike.
John is his Honda XR-100 dirt bike trying desperately to find his place
and fit in as one of the 'big boys'.

In reality the bike is small, tinny and flimsy
with a whiney engine. The pure mechanical manifestation
of all his teenage angst
and John is riding himself for his life.

The T-1000
is in hot pursuit.
John is not daft. He knows when to run.
The tow truck pursues the dirt bike.
Closing the gap,
gaining speed,
licking the rear wheel and preparing to feast.

We, the audience, hear a growl. Low like distant thunder
as the good Terminator arrives in the nick of time
to save John from his nefarious assailant.

The good Terminator rides a 1990 Harley-Davidson 'Fat Boy'
and by God has this thing got some power. A real grown-up.
Everything the Honda could ever dream to be.

This is the turning point.
John has arrived at the proverbial crunch.
With no time left
the good Terminator lifts John from the Honda
to place him safely onto the 'Fat Boy'
with no choice but to let go of
the one thing in the world that was him. His identifier and avatar
wobbles, oscillates and falls victim to the underside of
the tow truck,
succumbing to the end with a pathetic crunch.

This is where John Connor dies.

Everything that made John Connor
John Connor dies along with the crunch
and John never looks back.
John is reborn to become something greater than himself
and from that point on in the movie
John's future is not set.
There is no fate but what he makes for himself.

Level up

The beast was engulfed in flames.
It snarled at the boy
who stood on the precipice of Hell's canyon
glaring back into its face.
His heartbeat tore away at a pace
that was wild and daring.
He knew that it scared him
and though every fibre of his being told him to run
he ignored it.
He was through with despairing.
Only one could exist – they both knew this –
and each was determined to defeat their adversary.

But the boy was prepared!
He was ready!
He would fight to his very last breath
before Death came and took his last lungful of air.
He swallowed.
His throat was raw but his eyes were keen
and his mind was wary
and as the sweat dripped
he gripped tight to the shield and sword by his side
and ran

straight for the beast.
As the flames licked
and the brimstone kicked
there was no time to think
and even less for regrets.
He raced for the edge of the canyon depths.
He held his sword high,
screamed
and leapt.

We are the people who sit at traffic lights

We are the people who sit at traffic lights.
We wait for change while avoiding eye contact.
The awkward exchange of a glance sideways
in the carriageway interpreted wrong.

"Get off my case!"
"You're in the wrong lane!"
"She's pushing in!"
"You moron!"
"Imbecile!"
"Sweet Christ! INDICATE!"

We move at a snail's pace
and want to get home
to a calmer place. Yet here we stay
unable to escape this gridlock. This shambles.
The road like brambles
and it's only ten to eight.

We weren't promised this.
To waste away
but still it's ok
For the Radio 2 breakfast show to count down the days
till we can drink our wage.
We are blinkered.
Funnelled.
Kept in our place.

I can't breathe.
I am encased in a three door hatchback Citeroen coffin.
When I sit at the lights I am nothing.

But...

when I sit at the lights
the lights help me see
that everyone wants change.
Not just me.

Horses in the wake

I couldn't tell you where the wave broke.
I don't remember when or how
but we eventually caved in.
Look at us now.
We shattered.
We were exhausted.
I still feel it each time my foot
lands on the doorstep.
Bandaged. A war vet.

Do you feel it too? Do we still connect?
Or would you rather forget everything we went through?

Funny thing is
I can't remember half of the stuff that we did
but I do know this.

For a short while in a pocket of time
we were alive.
We were horses in the wake.
Thundering. Fearless.
An oncoming storm.
No rhyme or reason.
Void of form.
Defective and flawless.
We had each other and
we had it all.

For a time
we were unstoppable

and if there's nothing to show for it
I'll be the first to throw a handful of soil
on whatever remains
of this metaphorical end of days.
I will live with the wound and make out
it's a graze
but I will be damned if it's put down to a passing phase.
Because those were the days.
The best of our lives.
When we were nineteen
we were alive.

Farewell Honalee

Jackie never said goodbye.

He just, one day,

stopped coming

to play.

The sun stopped shining.

The grass turned grey and

nobody danced

on the days that it rained.

The kings and the princes

shut tight the gates

and the pirates were gone

with the next good wave.

The wind was too sad

to sing songs anymore

and the heartbroken dragon

forgot how to roar.

Can you remember?

Can you remember?

See if you can.

Those days when you weren't

a grown woman or man.

When life wasn't work

and you weren't in demand

and the perks of the day

outweighed all the bland

mechanical plans

that someone else made

for you to follow

so you could get paid.

And like a robot

you obeyed.

Can you remember the tune to your song?

The beat of your heart?

Or are you too far gone?

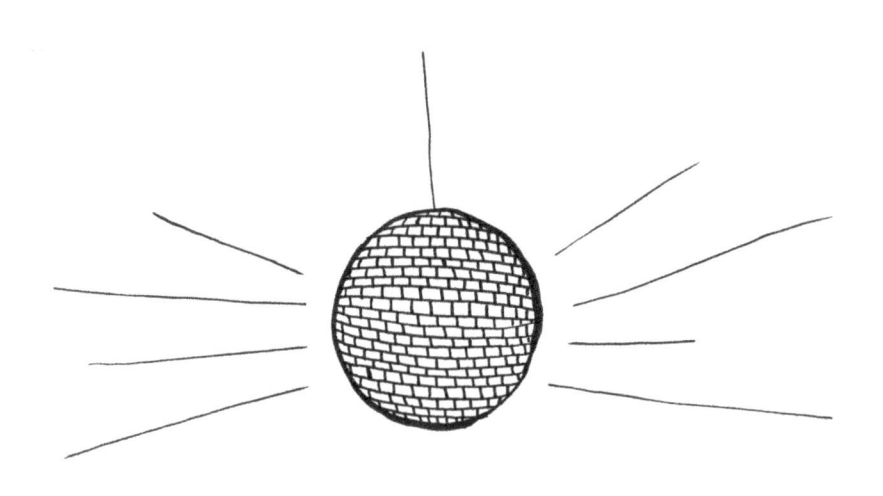

— I WILL KEEP DANCING —

"There could be fewer days ahead than gone
and all I've spent are long since on my way
to learning nothing comes for free"

- Ben Folds -

Tea

Just as the Librarians of the British Library
turn the pages of da-Vinci's notebooks.

With the same care and precision as a surgeon
performing a septal myectomy.

In the same way a ballet dancer graces the stage
with a touch as light as an angel's first kiss

and with all the buoyancy and weightlessness
of a Mint Aero bar
or a packet of Quavers

does my first cup of tea
welcome me into the day.

If Heaven exists then surely this is it?
With every sip I taste a bit..
I am not worthy
to drink such bliss
yet here I sit..

At my kitchen table..

Being gently lowered into another beautiful day.

The flowers are blooming, the sun is shining
and the birds are singing just for me.

Today will be a good day.
I will tackle it my way.
This is okay.

Dear Tom Gorman,
For one year you were my tutor at Birmingham University.
I'm almost certain that you don't remember me.
I was a mess. Long hair and no sense and
though I can barely remember studying
I do remember you.
We would spend breaks outside the old drama building in Selly Oak
smoking Mayfair brand cigarettes
till our lungs forgot what fresh air tasted like
and it was fabulous
and though I would never say it,
I really admired you.
In my eyes you were the epitome of cool. God tier.
You were a film buff and we'd talk sci-fi, cartoons and nerdy stuff
and you had this love for Sailor Moon
(which is generally seen as a girls cartoon)
but you embraced it.
We spent lunch times debating which was the best of the three
Star Wars movies and no matter what we decided at least we agreed
that of the Star Wars movies there are only three.
Original trilogy forever.
For me it was a place and time where I didn't quite fit
but I loved the lessons I had with you.
You were a fountain of knowledge and you oozed style
and I guess I was kind of jealous for a while and I think that maybe
I've subconsciously based a bit of who I am today
on what I remember of you.
I don't remember the last time I saw you.
I just remember that you left to go and work somewhere else and
everyone was pretty upset.

I'm a teacher now too.
I teach Early Years in Lancaster and when I'm not teaching I'm a performance poet. It's cool. I really enjoy it.
Anyway, I'm only writing this because when I moved house I recently found your copy of the soundtrack to the Buffy the Vampire Slayer musical episode.
'Once More With Feeling!'
I doubt you remember lending it to me
but I still listen to it from time to time.
It has this nostalgic magic. If I ever bump into you I'll give it back.
Anyway,
I hope you're well.
Ben

Evolve

I am like a hard drive
with unlimited space.
Void of anything
but consciousness.
I know I exist.
My heartbeat tells me this.
That I am here.
That I am me.
That I can evolve

from a blank slate.
A state of nothingness
with a deep,
insatiable hunger
to learn.
There is a brain to be filled.

I yearn
for knowledge.
I thirst for facts and figures.
I crave to experience as much as I can
and above all else I demand
to feel
the things I cannot understand.
I want to challenge myself
to rewire myself
so I can make sense of my world.

I want..
I want new.
I want to experience new without forgetting the old.
To wipe the things that make me me would break my heart.

I want to place my 'old' in a glass cabinet.
To display my being
and dead centre in a spotlight would be
all those times it went horribly wrong
right next to the times it went wonderfully right.
All the times that I stood strong
and the times I shattered would be on display

for all to see
and beneath would be a plaque
that reads
"I am proud of who I was.
I am proud of who I am today
and I can't wait to see
the person I become".

I will keep on dancing

It's strange
because I know what I want to say.

I have all the conversations intricately laid out in my head
like I've recorded our favourite tracks
on to a cassette and
I keep rewinding it like I'm rehearsing a play.

It's a mix tape of things you'll never get to hear
and I know exactly what I want to say,
I do,
but when I come to say it
I don't have the words to put it into words.
I just have these feelings that are so strong
and I feel like I'm constantly winded.

I never see you anymore.

I have photographs and memories but it's not the same.
I want to hold you. I want to feel that you are real
and I want to tell you that I love you
and I can't
and it hurts so bad.

I am being carved up from the inside because
I miss you.
You are my brother
and I love you.
I love you so, so much
and sometimes it feels like I can't contain all this love
and somehow
it's all here inside me
and it wants to burst out like a champagne cork.

There will never be another you
and like Cinderella you made sure
that no one else could fill your shoes
and you left us all at the ball.

Well, I will keep on dancing. Just for you.

You are my brother
and we are far apart
and though you are so very heavy,
I will carry you
forever
in my heart.

Beginning

Everything is packed.
We're ready to leave.
Sandwiches wrapped,
a scarf,
a hat,
a torch,
a compass,
a battered old map
and tea in a flask.
It's all compact
in the bag that's strapped
to the back of my back
but..
are you sure?
You do know that
once we go there's no turning back.
This is the last time we'll be here
but we'll not leave the past.
We'll store it up here.
For better. For worse.
Look, don't fear. I'll always be near
and together we'll steer our way
through the deepest and darkest caves.
We'll just be brave.
Together? OK?
I'm terrified too, but we'll find the way.

The future is white.
Behind us is grey.
I know,
sometimes it's better to say nothing at all
and if that's your way then that's your call.
Just let me put my hand in yours.
We'll support each other
and we won't fall.
We just need to step beyond this door.
One deep breath.
Count to four.
The future is ours.
Let's take it all.

Lightning Source UK Ltd.
Milton Keynes UK
UKHW052334080320
359955UK00007B/52